OKAY, ALL YOU WORD-TWISTING, SECRET-WRIT-
ING CODEBREAKERS OUT THERE, BET YOU CAN'T
FIGURE OUT WHAT THIS MEANS:

KEE POFF THEG RASS

SO YOU GUESSED RIGHT? BIG DEAL. BET YOU
CAN'T CRACK EITHER OF THESE TWO CODES:

TXFBUFST

OR

SAY WHAT? YOU HAVEN'T GOT A CLUE! WELL,
CODES, SIGNS, SYMBOLS, CLUES, AND ANSWERS
CAN ALL BE FOUND INSIDE! HAVE FUN!

JOIN THE GHOSTWRITER TEAM . . .

. . . on a tour of their Brooklyn neighborhood. As you go, you'll find there's something special about this place. From the street signs to the supermarket displays, the 'hood is full of puzzles and codes! Some of them were made up by the team; some of them were left by the team's mysterious friend, Ghostwriter—and some of them are as much a mystery to the team as they will be to you!

doubletalk

Codes,
Signs,
&
Symbols

A CHILDREN'S TELEVISION
WORKSHOP BOOK

by
HELENE
HOVANEC

Illustrated by
Chuck Wimmer

BANTAM BOOKS

NEW YORK • TORONTO • LONDON •
SYDNEY AUCKLAND

Doubletalk: Codes, Signs, and Symbols
A Bantam Book / November 1993

Ghostwriter, G**host**writer and ◉ are
trademarks of Children's Television Workshop.
All rights reserved. Used under authorization.

Art direction by Marva Martin
Cover art by Susan Herr
Interior illustrations by Chuck Wimmer

ISBN: 0–553–37218–1

Published simultaneously in the United States and Canada

Bantam Books are published by Bantam Books, a division of Bantam Doubleday Dell
Publishing Group, Inc. Its trademark, consisting of the words "Bantam Books" and the
portrayal of a rooster, is Registered in U.S. Patent and Trademark Office and in other
countries. Marca Registrada. Bantam Books, 1540 Broadway, New York, New York
10036.

PRINTED IN THE UNITED STATES OF AMERICA
OPM   0   9   8   7   6   5   4   3

Have you met the Ghostwriter team?

Jamal, Lenni, Alex, Gaby, Tina, and Rob. These New York kids have a hot secret: They're good friends with a ghost! Join them on a tour of their Brooklyn neighborhood. As you go, you'll find there's something special about this place. From the street signs to the supermarket displays, the 'hood is full of puzzles and codes! Some of them were made up by the team; some of them were left by the team's mysterious friend, Ghostwriter—and some of them are as much a mystery to the team as they will be to you!

Jamal **Lenni** **Alex**

Gaby **Tina** **Rob**

and GHOSTWRITER

Contents

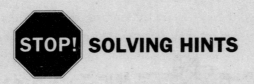

STOP! SOLVING HINTS

For an example of word searches, look at the grid below to see GABY and LENNI hidden horizontally; ALEX and ROB hidden vertically; and JAMAL and TINA hidden diagonally. ROB, LENNI, and JAMAL are written backward. Always circle the words carefully, because you'll have to put the leftover letters in spaces below the grid to find a hidden message.

Now write the extra letters from this grid above the lines below. Copy them in order from left to right, starting at the top. Soon you'll see the hidden message.

___ _____

____ __ ____!

-.. --- ..- -... .-.. . - .- .-.. -.-

To do word links, start by looking at the letters that are already in the grid. Look for a word on the list that contains one of the letters that's already filled in. Also, count the number of boxes that each word will take up.

In this grid JAMAL is already filled in. Look on the word list for a name that is four letters long *and* ends in the letter *A*. Got it? Add TINA to the grid and cross it off the list. Next, look on the list for a name that is five letters long and ends in *I*. Add LENNI to the grid and cross it off the list. Now you take over! Fill in the rest of the names and complete the word link.

ALEX	JAMAL	ROB
GABY	LENNI	TINA

1. EASY HARDWARE

The team was helping to build a new display case at the community center. Sally Lewis, the director, sent Lenni and Alex down to the hardware store to pick up some supplies. While Rob waited for them to come back, he made up this puzzle. Can you solve it? Add the tools listed below to the grid.

AWL	HATCHET	SANDER
BEVEL	HOE	SAW
DRILL	LATHE	SCREWDRIVER
EDGER	LEVEL	STAPLER
FILE	NAILS	VISE
HAMMER	PLIERS	WRENCH

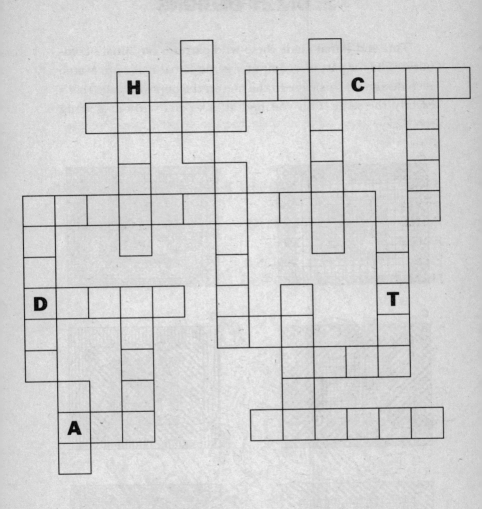

2. DIZZY DESIGNS

Tina and Jamal made these wild patterns on Jamal's computer. They're part of a computer game Jamal made up. Match each design on this page to the one on the opposite page that's exactly the same. Can you find all six pairs without getting too dizzy?

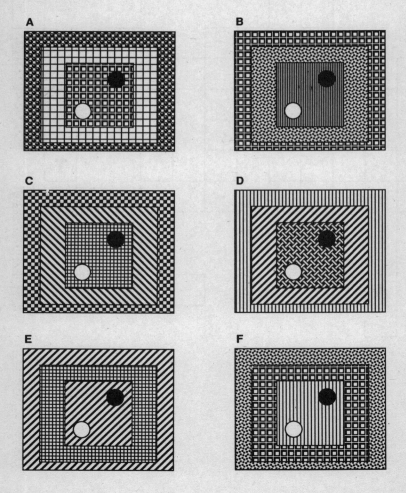

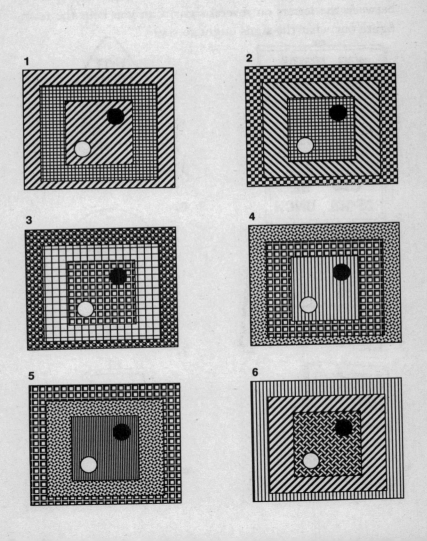

3. SIGNS OF THE TIMES

The kids on the Ghostwriter team were walking home from the community center when they noticed that Ghostwriter was playing a joke on them. He changed the spacing between the letters on several signs. Can you help the team figure out what the signs ought to say?

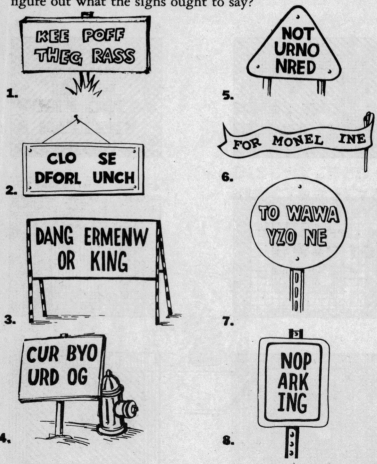

1. KEE POFF THEG RASS

2. CLO SE DFORL UNCH

3. DANG ERMENW OR KING

4. CUR BYO URD OG

5. NOT URNO NRED

6. FOR MONEL INE

7. TO WAWA YZO NE

8. NOP ARK ING

The team wanted to find out just what Ghostwriter could read, so they found two corny riddles and had Jamal print them out on his computer in an unusual way. Then Jamal typed a note to Ghostwriter: CAN YOU READ THESE?

NO, Ghostwriter wrote back. IS THIS SOME KIND OF CODE?

SORT OF, Jamal typed. YOU HAVE TO HOLD THEM UP TO A _ _ _ _ _ _.

Do you know how to read these riddles? Give it a try!

WHAT DID BEN FRANKLIN SAY WHEN HE DISCOVERED ELECTRICITY?

WHEN DOES A BATTERY GO SHOPPING?

WHEN IT RUNS OUT OF JUICE.

NOTHING, HE WAS TOO SHOCKED.

5. EXTRA LETTERS

Ghostwriter loves riddles. You have to have sharp eyes to solve this one, which he wrote on Jamal's computer. Both words on each line use the same letters *except* for one extra letter. Write that extra in the blank space. Then read *down* to answer this riddle: *What rides does Ghostwriter go on at amusement parks?*

WINTER _____ TWINE   POLISH _____ SPOIL

METEOR _____ METER   STOOPS _____ POSTS

CELLAR _____ CLEAR   SISTER _____ TIRES

CALLED _____ DECAL   PLANET _____ PLANE

CREATE _____ REACT   DESIRE _____ RIDES

SCRAPE _____ CAPES   TRIBES _____ BITES

RATING _____ TRAIN   STREAM _____ TAMER

16

6. CHECK IT OUT!

Lenni, Gaby, and Rob found a pile of funny books at the library. All the authors had names that had something to do with the titles of their books. Can you match each author with the book he or she wrote?

Draw a line from the author's name to his or her book.

Authors	Titles
Can D. Barr	*Diary of a Stuffed Animal*
C. Side	*Hup! Two, Three, Four . . .*
Ted E. Bear	*Don't Look Down! A Cliff-hanging Tale*
J. Walker	*How to Live on Another Planet*
Millie Terry	*101 Chocolate Goodies*
Dr. Ima Driller	*Sand in My Socks*
Prince E. Pal	*Don't Walk Now! How I Got Run Over by a Bus*
Eileen Dover	*Tales from the Dentist's Chair*
V. Ness	*How to Run a School—and Survive!*

7. PUZZLE OF THE YEAR

The Fort Greene library declared this year the Year of the Puzzle—so Lenni and Gaby decided to make the puzzle of the year! They filled in a few letters, then took a break. Can you finish it for them? Find the correct place in the grid for every month.

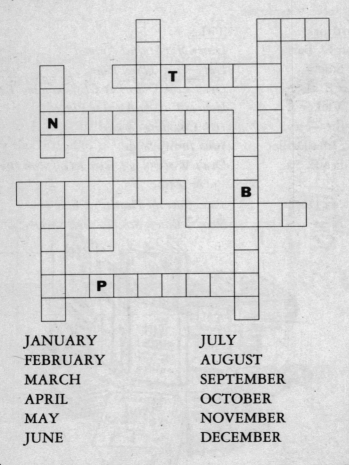

JANUARY

FEBRUARY

MARCH

APRIL

MAY

JUNE

JULY

AUGUST

SEPTEMBER

OCTOBER

NOVEMBER

DECEMBER

8. ANN T. NIM

The new book by Ann T. Nim finally arrived at the library! Nim writes Alex's favorite kind of books. What kind of books does Alex like? Well, solve the puzzle below and it won't be a mystery any longer!

To solve the puzzle:

- Find the opposite (*antonym*, get it?) of each word on the list. Write it in the grid, going *down*.
- When you've filled in all the spaces in the grid, read the third line across. It'll tell you what kind of person is the hero of Ann T. Nim's new book.

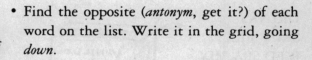

1	2	3	4	5	6	7	8	9
H								
I								
D								
E								

1.	SEEK	**4.**	ODD	**7.**	THAT
2.	UNDER	**5.**	POOR	**8.**	SPEND
3.	STANDS	**6.**	LOVE	**9.**	SHUT

9. SUPERMARKET MIX-UP

Jamal promised his mother he'd pick up some things from the supermarket, but when he got there he found that some joker had been there first. The joker changed just one letter on each sign—and made real products into fake ones!

Jamal's in a hurry to get the shopping done so that he can go to a rally at Lenni's place. Can you help him find the joke letters and change them back to what they should be?

DRINKS
SKIM SILK
ICED SEA MIX
BOOT BEER
FINGER ALE
GRANGE JUICE

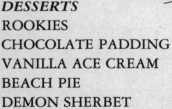

DESSERTS
ROOKIES
CHOCOLATE PADDING
VANILLA ACE CREAM
BEACH PIE
DEMON SHERBET

NONFOOD ITEMS
GARBAGE BUGS
PIPER TOWELS
OPEN CLEANER
LIQUID SNAP
PLASTIC TRAP

10. EXTRA! EXTRA!

Lenni and Tina wanted to help Jamal get his shopping done. They went to get meat and produce for him. But they found that the joker had been there before them! This time he added one extra letter to each item and made new words. Help Lenni and Tina by crossing out the letter in each line that doesn't belong. Tina did the first one already.

FRUITS & VEGETABLES

PREACHES

DAPPLES

SCORN

BERETS

SLIMES

PLEAS

PLUMES

MEAT & POULTRY

TURNKEY

STREAK

WHAM

SLIVER

PORK CHOMPS

CHICKEN SWINGS

BEACON

11. SANDWICH FIXINGS

Rob, Alex, Lenni, and Jamal rallied in the school cafeteria at lunch. They were on a case, and Rob had a new clue—but he didn't know what to make of it. Suddenly this message from Ghostwriter appeared on the lunch menu:

"Add all the sandwich items on the list to the puzzle grid. The item that doesn't fit into the grid will tell you what I think of this new clue."

BALONEY	PEPPER
CHEESE	ROAST BEEF
CHICKEN	SALAMI
HAM	SALT
LETTUCE	TOMATOES
MAYONNAISE	TURKEY
OIL	VINEGAR

Fill in the leftover word below to get Ghostwriter's message about the new clue:

IT'S __ __ __ __ __ __ __ !

-.. --- ..- -... .-.. .   - .- .-.. .-.

12. ANAGRAM LAND

Alex and Rob went to buy a map at the bookstore so that Alex could get a better idea of where his pen pals actually lived. They were checking out world maps when they noticed that CHINA had been changed to CHAIN. They knew that Ghostwriter was there, playing one of his favorite games with them: anagrams. Can you match each foreign country with the new word that Ghostwriter formed? Remember that in an anagram, all the letters of the original word are used in the new word.

CHINA

IRAN

NEPAL

NIGER

MALI

SPAIN

PERU

OMAN

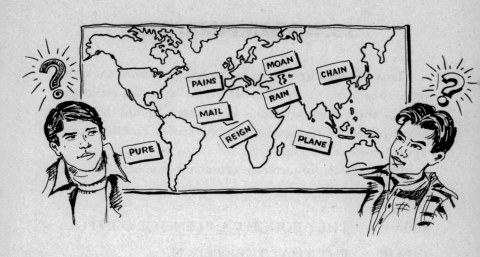

RAIN	**PAINS**	**REIGN**
MAIL	**CHAIN**	**PURE**
	PLANE	**MOAN**

13. HIDDEN FURNITURE

Tina was making a video and needed a chair as one of her props. She went to a thrift shop to see what she could get. But the thrift shop owner was a prankster. He hid the names of the pieces of furniture inside these sentences. Ghostwriter figured one out for Tina.

Using the list of furniture below, can you help Tina sort through the rest?

BED   THEY BOUGH<u>T A BLE</u>ND OF COFFEES.

CHAIR   PUT THAT TUBE DOWN.

COT   SHE ATE ONE TACO TODAY.

LAMP   WHICH AIRPORT IS CLOSE TO YOUR HOUSE?

SOFA   DON'T SLAM PAPA'S DOOR!

TABLE   WHY DO YOU WALK SO FAST?

-.. --- ..- -... .-.. . - .- .-.. -.-

14. TRACK IT DOWN

Gaby and Alex were going shopping and wanted to see if Ghostwriter could figure out what type of store they were going to. Help Ghostwriter find the store by adding all the listed words to the grid. Then read *down* the shaded column. Gaby and Alex put in a few letters for you.

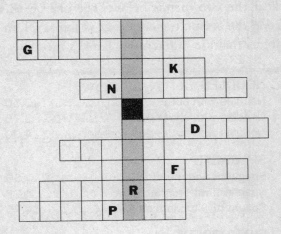

BOOTS
GALOSHES
LOAFERS
MOCCASINS
OXFORDS

SANDALS
SLIPPERS
SNEAKERS
SOCKS

15. MENU MESS

Lenni's dad, Max, took the whole team out to dinner on Lenni's birthday. Lenni, Rob, and Gaby shared one menu, while Jamal, Alex, and Tina shared another. Jamal's group kept cracking up. Someone had messed with their menu and given them some seriously weird food choices!

Look at the two menus below. The one on this page is Lenni's, and the one on the next page is Jamal's. Can you find the 12 items that are different on Jamal's menu?

NOODLES
Noodles with butter 3.50
Noodles with cheese 3.75
Noodles with butter and cheese 4.00

SPAGHETTI
Spaghetti and meatballs 4.50
Spaghetti with tomato sauce 4.25
Spaghetti with clam sauce 4.75

SIDE ORDERS
Onion rings 1.50
French fries 1.50

DRINKS
Soda 1.00
Coffee or tea 1.00
Root beer 1.25

DESSERTS
Ice cream 1.50
Pie 1.50
Pie à la mode 2.50

NOODLES
Noodles with batter 3.50
Poodles with cheese 3.75
Noodles with butter ant cheese 4.00

SPAGHETTI
Spaghetti and meatballs 4.50
Spaghetti with tomato sauce 4.25
Spaghetti with clay sauce 4.75

SIDE ORDERS
Union rings 1.50
French flies 1.50

DRINKS
Coda 1.00
Coffee or sea 1.00
Roof beer 1.25

DESSERTS
Ick cream 1.50
Tie 1.50
Pie à la mole 2.50

16. DOG WATCHING

Rob is hoping to get a dog. He and Alex went to the local pet shop, where they got an idea for a puzzle. Can you solve it? All the dog breeds listed below are hidden on the opposite page. Look forward, backward, up, down, and diagonally and circle each word as you find it. When you finish circling, take all the leftover letters and write them below the grid. Work carefully, copying the letters from left to right and top to bottom, to answer the riddle. Alex circled a word for you and crossed it off the list.

AFGHAN	COLLIE	POODLE
AIREDALE	~~DACHSHUND~~	PULI
BEAGLE	DALMATIAN	SALUKI
BOXER	LHASA APSO	SPANIEL
CHIHUAHUA	PEKINGESE	SPITZ

RIDDLE:
WHAT SHOULD YOU DO WITH NOISY DOGS WHEN YOU GO SHOPPING?

```
P E K I N G E S E D D
C O L L I E P A A A
H B O X E R U L T C
I E A D T H M U E H
H A F M L A I K S S
U G G N T E A I P H
A L H I P U L I A U
H E A B A R T K N N
U N N I N Z G L I D
A A I R E D A L E O
O S P A A S A H L T
```

ANSWER:

___ ___ ___ ___ ___ ___ ___ ___ ___ ___

___ ___ ___ ___ ___ ___ ___ ___ ___

___ ___ ___ ___ .

-.. --- ..- -... .-.. . ─ .- .-.. -.-

17. BIRD'S-EYE VIEW

When Jamal and Lenni heard what Rob and Alex had done they decided to come up with their own puzzle. Solve this puzzle the way you did Rob and Alex's dog puzzle.

CANARY   ORIOLE   RAVEN
CRANE   OWL   ROBIN
DOVE   PARAKEET   SWALLOW
EAGLE   PARROT   SWAN
FALCON   PELICAN   WOODPECKER
HAWK   PHEASANT
LARK   PIGEON

RIDDLE:
WHAT DO BIRDS SAY ON HALLOWEEN?

N C T N A S A E H P
A A T R I E L G A E
W N I B O R C R P L
S A N O C L A F I I
W R H A W K K V G C
A Y O R E D O V E A
L T W E L O I R O N
L E T C R A N E N E
O W L T T O R R A P
W O O D P E C K E R

ANSWER:

__ __ __ __ __ __ __

__ __ __ __ __ .

-.. --- ..- -... .-.. . - --. .-. -.. -.-

18. ANIMALSPEAK

Gaby and Tina noticed that a lot of everyday expressions make use of animals. Here are a few they thought of. Plug in the right animal for each sentence.

1. They're packed tight as_____in a can.

2. Put leftovers from a restaurant into a_____bag.

3. Do you like to_____out on junk food?

4. Some people use_____ears for a TV antenna.

5. He felt uncomfortable, like a_____out of water.

6. Hold your_____! Be calm.

7. Soldiers hide out in_____holes.

DOGGIE

FISH

FOX

HORSES

PIG

RABBIT

SARDINES

19. BAKE-OFF

Tina took her younger sister, Linda, to the bakery to pick out a treat. Linda wanted the sweetest thing she could find. While Linda was making up her mind Tina made up this word link. Can you fit all the baked goods on the list below into the grid?

BAGELS
BISCUITS
BREADS
BROWNIES

BUNS
CHEESECAKES
COOKIES

DOUGHNUTS
MUFFINS
SCONES

Now unscramble the letters in the shaded boxes to find out what Linda ended up getting. (Tina filled in two letters for you.)

A T _ _ _ _ _ _ C _ _

20. DEP ART MENTS TO RE

The whole team decided to do their holiday shopping together, so they went to a big department store. Jamal's sister, Danitra, went along with them. Since they all had different needs, they decided to read the signs that would help them, split up, do their shopping, and meet later. But the writing on all the signs was spaced wrong. From the information given below, can you match up each person to a sign? And can you tell who couldn't go into the department store?

1. Tina and Gaby are pooling their money to buy a dress for Lenni.
2. Lenni wants to buy a doll for her cousin.
3. Alex wants to have his purchase wrapped.
4. Rob wants to get a new shirt for his dad.
5. Danitra is walking her friend's poodle.
6. Jamal won't walk up more than three flights of stairs.

-.. --- ..- -... .-.. . - .- .-.. -.-

EL E VAT
ORT OTH
EFIF THF
LOOR

Dre
ssesf
orj uni
ors

NOD OG
SALL O
WED

BO OK
SAND
TO YS

GI FTW
RAPDE
P ART
ME NT

21. CLOTHES CODE

When Tina reached the clothing department she noticed that all the signs were written in code. Suddenly she saw a message from Ghostwriter: "I know how to break this code! Just change each letter to the one that comes before it in the alphabet."

Can you help Tina read each coded sign? To help you out, here's a copy of the alphabet.

A B C D E F G H I J K L M N O P Q R S T U V W X Y Z

ESFTTFT __ __ __ __ __ __ __

IBUT __ __ __ __

KBDLFUT __ __ __ __ __ __ __

QBKBNBT __ __ __ __ __ __ __

SBJODPBUT __ __ __ __ __ __ __ __ __

SPCFT __ __ __ __ __

TIJSUT __ __ __ __ __ __

TIPFT __ __ __ __ __

TLJSUT __ __ __ __ __ __

TPDLT __ __ __ __ __

TVJUT __ __ __ __ __

TXFBUFST __ __ __ __ __ __ __ __

UJFT __ __ __ __

WFTUT __ __ __ __ __

22. GOOD SPORTS

Gaby and Jamal met at the sporting goods store to buy new karate uniforms, which are known as "gi." Gaby changed a letter in each sign to see if she could confuse Jamal—or at least make him laugh!

Can you figure out what the right words are?

BOWLING BAWL

HOCKEY SLICK

HIGH-TOP SPEAKERS

BOXING CLOVES

BUNCHING BAG

BASEBALL BUT

SHOULDER PODS

VOLLEYBALL NOT

KARATE GO

23. CUT IT OUT

Lenni's dad gave her a list of items he needed from the drugstore. But when Lenni got to the store she found that someone had cut a word out of each sign. Help Lenni do her shopping by placing one of the words on the right into an empty space on the left to complete each sign.

____IRINS	AIR
____TAL FLOSS	ANT
DEODOR____	TOO
H____SPRAY	DEN
M____HWASH	HAM
S____POO	HOW
S____ER CAP	OUT
TIS____S	ASP
____THPASTE	SUE

24. TOSSED SALAD

Gaby and Alex were in their family's bodega when Gaby noticed that the letters on the signs on the vegetable stand were scrambling like crazy. Ghostwriter! Gaby wrote him a note, asking him what he was doing.

"Making tossed salad!" Ghostwriter wrote back.

Can you unscramble the tossed words and find out what kind of vegetables are in Ghostwriter's salad?

LUCETTE   _ _ _ _ _ _ _

IONONS   _ _ _ _ _ _

MATOESOT   _ _ _ _ _ _ _ _

LERYEC   _ _ _ _ _ _

STARROC   _ _ _ _ _ _ _

CAPSHIN   _ _ _ _ _ _ _

NABES   _ _ _ _ _

CORCBOLI   _ _ _ _ _ _ _ _

25. NOTABLE NOTE

One day Gaby found a torn-up note on her brother Alex's desk. When she started to piece it together, she got the shock of her life! Quickly she wrote to Ghostwriter: "Help! Alex is trying to kill me! What should I do?"

But when Ghostwriter read the note, he told Gaby she was wrong. Alex wasn't trying to kill her. Gaby just hadn't looked at all the evidence.

Can you piece together Alex's note and figure out what it really says?

-.. --- ..- -... .-.. . - .- .-.. -.-

26. SPACED OUT

Gaby's favorite superhero is Galaxy Girl. Rob wrote this story about Galaxy Girl's space adventures just for Gaby. And to make it more fun, he built a puzzle into it!

Galaxy Girl was on the street in BROOKLYN one day when a small, SAUCER-shaped SPACESHIP suddenly landed in front of her. The hatch opened and out popped two tiny green people.

The first one turned to the second one. "Where are we?" it asked. "This looks like PLANET Quezenflanj."

The second creature pointed to a street sign. "You dummy! Can't you read? We're on Planet De Kalb AVENUE."

Galaxy Girl burst out laughing.

The tiny green creatures jumped. "Eep!" the first one squeaked. "It's a talking MOUNTAIN!"

"I'm not a mountain," Galaxy Girl told them. "I'm Galaxy Girl. Welcome to Planet EARTH!"

To solve Rob's puzzle, find the words in the story that are all in CAPITAL LETTERS. Fit them into the correct spaces in the grid, going *across*. Then read *down* the shaded boxes to find the answer to this riddle:

What is Galaxy Girl's favorite TV channel?

Rob filled in a few letters to get you started.

44   -..   ---   ..-   -...   .-..   .   -   .-   .-..   -.-

-.. --- ..- -... .-. . - .- .-. -.- 45

27. LOST IN SPICE

Mr. Fernandez, Gaby and Alex's father, ordered some spices for his bodega from a new supplier. But when the order was delivered, he found that all the labels had been torn. Help Gaby and Alex figure out where the torn pieces belong.

GA	C	CURR		**BAS**	
LL		**SAF**	N	*INT*	
CHI		P	PER	LT	
CIN	ON	*TAR*	*ON*	MA	*RAM*
S	**GE**	*FEN*	L	**PA**	**LEY**

Y   *RLI*   *SA*

RJO   **IL**   *NE*

DI   *EP*   **LI**

FRO   NAM   *RAG*

RS   *M*   **A**

28. SYMBOL CODE

Gaby collected a bunch of ghost jokes in her fact book, planning to surprise Ghostwriter. She kept them in a secret code so that Ghostwriter couldn't read them in advance.

In Gaby's code, each symbol stands for one letter of the alphabet. Replace each symbol on the opposite page with the correct letter and you'll find a riddle and its answer! Here's the first one.

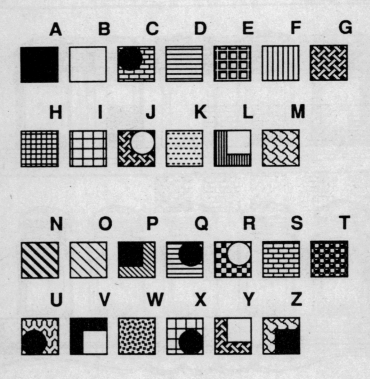

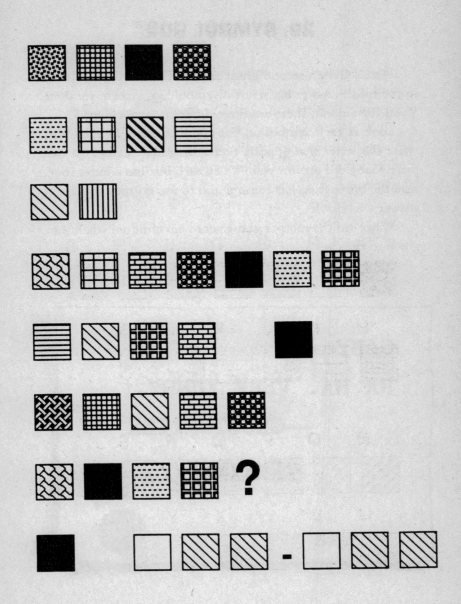

29. SYMBOL BOX

Here's Gaby's second ghost riddle. This time, each letter in the riddle answer has its own symbol. So, if there are three *S*'s in the answer, there are three different symbols for *S*.

Look at each symbol on the opposite page. In each box, write the letter that appears under the same symbol on this page. Gaby did one for you. When each box has a letter in it, read the boxes from left to right and top to bottom and you'll answer this riddle:

What did the mother ghost say to her children when they got into the car?

```
GABY--

  HA HA. VERY FUNNY.

     --GHOSTWRITER

        XXXXXXXXX...
```

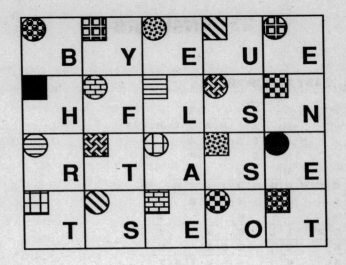

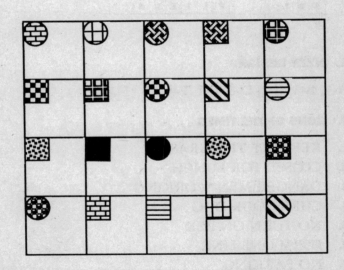

ANSWERS

1. EASY HARDWARE

```
        F         S
     H  I      H A T C H E T
   N A I L S          A       D
     M    E  W        P       G
 S C R E W D R I V E R        E
 A    R       E       R   L   R
 N    D       N       C   A
 D R I L L    C   B       T
 E    E       H O E       H
 R               V I S E
   S  E
   A  W L     P L I E R S
   W
```

2. DIZZY DESIGNS

A-3, B-5, C-2, D-6, E-1, F-4

3. SIGNS OF THE TIMES

1. KEEP OFF THE GRASS
2. CLOSED FOR LUNCH
3. DANGER MEN WORKING
4. CURB YOUR DOG
5. NO TURN ON RED
6. FORM ONE LINE
7. NO PARKING
8. TOW AWAY ZONE
9. SCHOOL BUS STOP

-.. --- ..- -... .-.. . - .- .-.. -.-

4. ЯOЯЯIM ,ЯOЯЯIM *HINT:* HOLD THE PAGE UP TO A MIRROR.

WHEN DOES A BATTERY GO SHOPPING? When it runs out of juice.

WHAT DID BEN FRANKLIN SAY WHEN HE DISCOVERED ELECTRICITY? Nothing, he was too shocked.

5. EXTRA LETTERS

WINTER	R	TWINE
METEOR	O	METER
CELLAR	L	CLEAR
CALLED	L	DECAL
CREATE	E	REACT
SCRAPE	R	CAPES
RATING	G	TRAIN
POLISH	H	SPOIL
STOOPS	O	POSTS
SISTER	S	TIRES
PLANET	T	PLANE
DESIRE	E	RIDES
TRIBES	R	BITES
STREAM	S	TAMER

ANSWER : ROLLER GHOSTERS!

6. CHECK IT OUT!

101 Chocolate Goodies by Can D. Barr

Sand in My Socks by C. Side

Diary of a Stuffed Animal by Ted. E. Bear

Don't Walk Now! How I Got Run Over by a Bus by J. Walker.

Hup! Two, Three, Four . . . by Millie Terry

Tales from the Dentist's Chair by Dr. Ima Driller

-.. --- ..- -... .-.. . - .- .-.. -.- 53

How to Run a School—and Survive! by Prince E. Pal
Don't Look Down! A Cliff-hanging Tale by Eileen Dover
How to Live on Another Planet by V. Ness

7. PUZZLE OF THE YEAR

```
            D                   M A Y
            E                   A
    J       O C T O B E R       R
    U       E                   C
    N O V E M B E R             H
    E       B             F
            E       J     E
    J A N U A R Y         B
    U       L       A P R I L
    G       Y             U
    U                     A
    S E P T E M B E R     R
    T                     Y
```

8. ANN T. NIM

H	O	S	E	R	H	T	S	O
I	V	I	V	I	A	H	A	P
D	E	T	E	C	T	I	V	E
E	R	S	N	H	E	S	E	N

9. SUPERMARKET MIX-UP

Drinks
SKIM MILK
ICED TEA MIX
ROOT BEER
GINGER ALE
ORANGE JUICE

Desserts
COOKIES
CHOCOLATE PUDDING
VANILLA ICE CREAM
PEACH PIE
LEMON SHERBET

Nonfood Items
GARBAGE BAGS
PAPER TOWELS
OVEN CLEANER
LIQUID SOAP
PLASTIC WRAP

10. EXTRA! EXTRA!

Fruits & Vegetables
PEACHES
APPLES
CORN
BEETS
LIMES
PEAS
PLUMS

Meat & Poultry
TURKEY
STEAK
HAM
LIVER
PORK CHOPS
CHICKEN WINGS
BACON

-.. --- ..- -... .-.. . - .- .-.. -.- 55

11. SANDWICH FIXINGS

```
        H     T           O     L
      M A Y O N N A I S E       L E
        M     M           L     T T
              A                 T U
      R O A S T B E E F         U C
              O                 C E
          C H E E S E           E
  S       H     S     A     P
  A       I           L     E
  L       C           A     P
  T U R K E Y         M     P
          E       V I N E G A R
          N                 R
```

ANSWER: IT'S BALONEY

12. ANAGRAM LAND

China   Chain
Iran   Rain
Mali   Mail
Nepal   Plane
Niger   Reign
Oman   Moan
Spain   Pains
Peru   Pure

13. HIDDEN FURNITURE

THEY BOUGH*T A BLE*ND OF COFFEES.
PUT THAT *TUBE D*OWN.
SHE ATE ONE *TACO* TODAY.
WHI*CH AIR*PORT IS CLOSE TO YOUR HOUSE?
DON'T S*LAM PAPA'S* DOOR!
WHY DO YOU WALK *SO FAST*?

56   -..   ---   ..-   -...   .-..   .   -   .-   .-..   -.-

14. TRACK IT DOWN

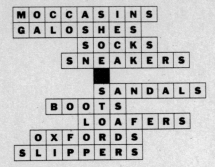

ANSWER: SHOE STORE

15. MENU MESS

NOODLES
Noodles with **batter**
Poodles with cheese
Noodles with butter **ant** cheese

SPAGHETTI
Spaghetti with **clay** sauce

SIDE ORDERS
Union rings
French **flies**

DRINKS
Coda
Coffee or **sea**
Roof beer

DESSERTS

Ick cream

Tie

Pie à la mole

16. DOG WATCHING

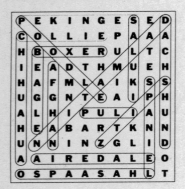

ANSWER: PUT THEM IN A BARKING LOT

17. BIRD'S-EYE VIEW

ANSWER: TRICK OR TWEET

-.. --- ..- -... .-.. . - .- .-.. -.-

18. ANIMALSPEAK

1. SARDINES
2. DOGGIE
3. PIG
4. RABBIT
5. FISH
6. HORSES
7. FOX

19. BAKE-OFF

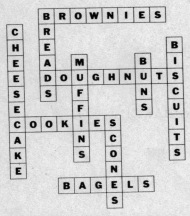

ANSWER: A TOOTHACHE

20. DEP ART MENTS TO RE

1-C, 2-E, 3-F, 4-A, 5-D, 6-B
Danitra couldn't go into the store because no dogs are allowed.

21. CLOTHES CODE

DRESSES
HATS

JACKETS
RAINCOATS
ROBES
SHIRTS
SHOES
SKIRTS
SOCKS
SUITS
SWEATERS
TIES
VESTS

22. GOOD SPORTS

BOWLING BALL
HOCKEY STICK
HIGH-TOP SNEAKERS
BOXING GLOVES
PUNCHING BAG
BASEBALL BAT
SHOULDER PADS
VOLLEYBALL NET
KARATE GI

23. CUT IT OUT

ASPIRINS
DENTAL FLOSS
DEODORANT
HAIR SPRAY
MOUTHWASH
SHAMPOO

-.. --- ..- -... .-.. . - .- .-.. -.-

SHOWER CAP
TISSUES
TOOTHPASTE

24. TOSSED SALAD

LETTUCE
ONIONS
TOMATOES
CELERY
CARROTS
SPINACH
BEANS
BROCCOLI

25. NOTABLE NOTE

Hey Tina—

I'm going to shoot some hoops
after school. I have tons of homework
but do you want to catch
a movie? I think Gaby
is trying to work it out
so that she can make it
too.

Later,

Alex

26. SPACED OUT

```
        M O U N T A I N
    E A R T H
        A V E N U E
    P L A N E T
B R O O K L Y N
        S A U C E R
  S P A C E S H I P
```

ANSWER: M TVENUS

27. LOST IN SPICE

GARLIC	CURRY	**BASIL**
DILL	**SAFFRON**	*MINT*
CHILI	PEPPER	SALT
CINNAMON	*TARRAGON*	*MARJORAM*
SAGE	*FENNEL*	**PARSLEY**

28. SYMBOL CODE

What kind of mistake does a ghost make? A boo-boo.

29. SYMBOL BOX

Fasten your sheet belts.

-.. --- ..- -... .-.. . - .- .-.. -.-

WATCH IT! SOLVE IT! TELL A FRIEND!

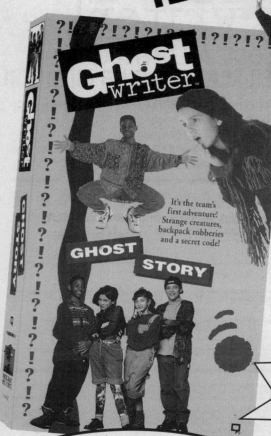

It's the team's first adventure! Strange creatures, backpack robberies and a secret code!

Ghostwriter Is Now Available On Videocassette!

$14.98* EACH
*Suggested Retail Price

FREE! Cool **Ghost writer** Puzzles inside each cassette!

From the
Hit TV Show

ghost writer

Created by CTW

BECOME AN OFFICIAL
GHOSTWRITER READERS CLUB MEMBER!

You'll receive the following GHOSTWRITER Readers Club Materials:
Official Membership Card • The Scoop on GHOSTWRITER •
GHOSTWRITER Magazine
All members registered by December 31st will have a chance to win
a FREE COMPUTER and other exciting prizes!

O F F I C I A L   E N T R Y   F O R M

Mail your completed entry to: Bantam Doubleday Dell BFYR,
GW Club, 1540 Broadway, New York, NY 10036

Name

Address

City   **State**   **Zip**

Age   **Phone**

Club Sweepstakes Official Rules
1. No purchase necessary. Enter by completing and returning the Entry Coupon. All entries must be received by Bantam Doubleday Dell no later than December 31, 1993. No mechanically reproduced entries allowed. By entering the sweepstakes, each entrant agrees to be bound by these rules and the decision of the judges which shall be final and binding. Limit: one entry per person.
2. The prizes are as follows: Grand Prize: One computer with monitor (approximate retail value of Grand Prize $3,000), First Prizes: Ten GHOSTWRITER libraries (approximate retail value of each First Prize: $25), Second Prizes: Five GHOSTWRITER backpacks (approximate retail value of each Second Prize: $25), and Third Prizes: Ten GHOSTWRITER T-Shirts (approximate retail value of each Third Prize: $10). Winners will be chosen in a random drawing on or about January 10, 1994, from among all completed Entry Coupons received and will be notified by mail. Odds of winning depend on the number of entries received. No substitution or transfer of the prize is allowed. All entries become property of BDD and will not be returned. Taxes, if any, are the sole responsibility of the winner. BDD reserves the right to substitute a prize of equal or greater value if any prize becomes unavailable.
3. This sweepstakes is open only to the residents of the U.S. and Canada, excluding the Province of Quebec, who are between the ages of 6 and 14 at the time of entry. The winner, if Canadian, will be required to answer correctly a time-limited arithmetical skill testing question in order to receive the prize. Employees of Bantam Doubleday Dell Publishing Group Inc. and its subsidiaries and affiliates and their immediate family members are not eligible. Void where prohibited or restricted by law. Grand and first prize winners will be required to execute and return within 14 days of notification an affidavit of eligibility and release to be signed by winner and winner's parent or legal guardian. In the event of noncompliance with this time period, an alternate winner will be chosen.
4. Entering the sweepstakes constitutes permission for use of the winner's name, likeness, and biographical data for publicity and promotional purposes on behalf of BDD, with no additional compensation. For the name of the winner, available after January 31, 1994, send a self-addressed envelope, entirely separate from your entry, to Bantam Doubleday Dell, BFYR Marketing Department, 1540 Broadway, New York, NY 10036.

FUNNY FIRSTS™

MY CAT IS GOING TO THE DOGS

by Mike Thaler • pictures by Jared Lee

Meow.

Troll Associates

**For Dr. Andre Ross,
who always had
strange things in her icebox!
M.T.**

**To my daughter Jana
who loves animals
J.L.**

Library of Congress Cataloging-in-Publication Data

Thaler, Mike, (date)
   My cat is going to the dogs / by Mike Thaler; pictures by Jared
Lee.
     p.   cm.—(Funny Firsts)
   Summary: A young boy worries about what will happen to his sick
cat when he takes it to the veterinarian for the first time.
   ISBN 0-8167-3022-9 (lib. bdg.)   ISBN 0-8167-3023-7 (pbk.)
   [1. Veterinarians—Fiction. 2. Cats—Fiction.] I. Lee, Jared
D., ill. II. Title. III. Series.
PZ7.T3Mt 1994
[E]—dc20   93-18596

My cat, Max, is sick.

He got real fat, and doesn't want to play. I didn't know cats got sick just like people.

Do other animals get sick, too? Do weasels get measles?

Do porcupines get pimples?

Do frogs get people in their throats?

Mom says we're taking Max to a veterinarian—a doctor just for animals.

Do the animals sit in the waiting room and read magazines just like we do? Is the nurse an aardvark?

I wonder if the whole zoo will be at the
doctor's office. Maybe we'll see an
elephant with a cold,

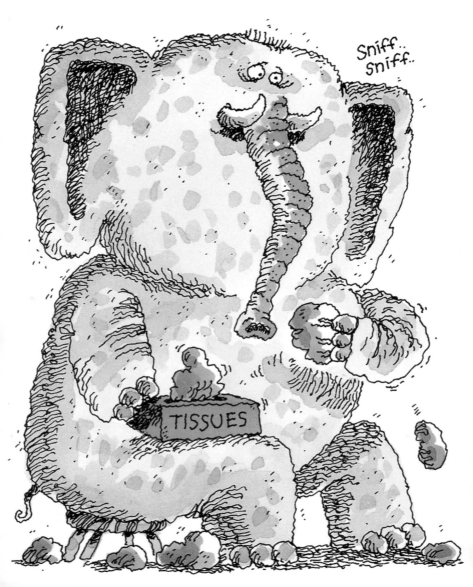

or a giraffe with a sore throat,

or a zebra with a sunburn.

Maybe there will be an alligator with a toothache,

or a big snake with a bellyache.

I wonder if the doctor treats the animals just like people?

I've heard that doctors do experiments on animals.

I won't let him hurt you, Max.

There are no unusual animals in the
waiting room, just a girl with a dog.
The dog looks scared.

Then out comes the nurse.
She's not an aardvark!

They go in and close the door.
Suddenly, there are horrible noises!

Then out they come. The dog's on crutches, and we're next!

We go into the room. There are all sorts of strange things in bottles. Will Max wind up in a bottle?

The doctor comes in. He pats Max on the head. Then he puts on rubber gloves and looks in Max's ears. I wonder what he's looking for?

Then he looks in Max's eyes and in his mouth. I guess he didn't find it in his ears.

Then he listens to Max's heart. I'm getting very nervous. Will Max have to go to the hospital? Will he die?

Then he gently pats Max's stomach and smiles. When he tells us the news, even Max looks surprised.

Guess what? The vet was right.
A week later, Max had four kittens.

So I changed his name to Maxine.

Mom let me keep all the kittens.

And, if they ever get sick, I'm going to take them to my friend . . .

Dr. Beagle, the vet!